Ethan's Healthy Mind Express
A Children's First Mental Health Primer

© 2019 Ethan Bean Mental Wellness Foundation
Farmington Hills, MI. All Rights Reserved.

By Emily Lane Waszak and Erik Bean, Ed.D.

Editor, Sherry Wexler

Illustrations, Gail Gorske

Jacket Design, Chris Calabrese

ISBN: 978-0-692-03655-6

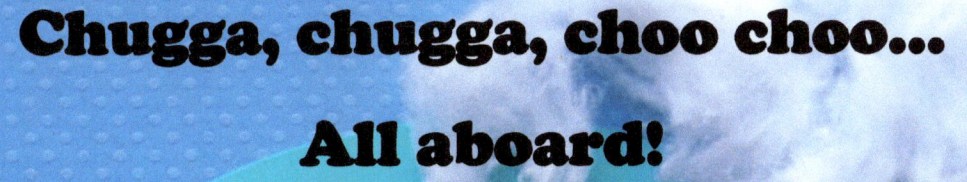

Chugga, chugga, choo choo...
All aboard!

FRIENDS
FAITH
FAMILY

SCHOOL
COMMUNITY
MEDIA

403

Ethan's Healthy Mind Express
is the place to be;
all aboard the trusty
Engine 403.

Some tracks are bumpy
or smooth or narrow or wide,
but all tracks will end up on
a magnificent ride.

Everyone is welcome
on the 403:
moms, dads, brothers, sisters,
even you and even me!

Our Healthy Mind Conductor
will lead the way.
He will guide us
toward a better day.

The 403 Express leads the town
to get on the right track,
getting help for us all
while not looking back.

It's an exciting ride
about to begin,
making new friends,
exploring feelings within.

There are many emotions
all on display.
People feel different
every single day.

You can't always tell
when something is wrong.
Some are quite weak
even though they look strong.

Rena boards first.
She struggles every day.
She doesn't even know
why she feels this way.

Some days she's happy.
Others, she's real sad.
She changes her moods often
which makes her feel bad.

Some friends might struggle
while learning in school.
They need extra help
and that feels uncool.

Teachers teach.
Friends help with studies.
Working together,
we can all be buddies.

Evan needs help to learn
no matter how hard he tries.
His brain works differently
than most other guys.

He wants to know everything
the teacher has to say,
but it's hard to pay attention
in class every day.

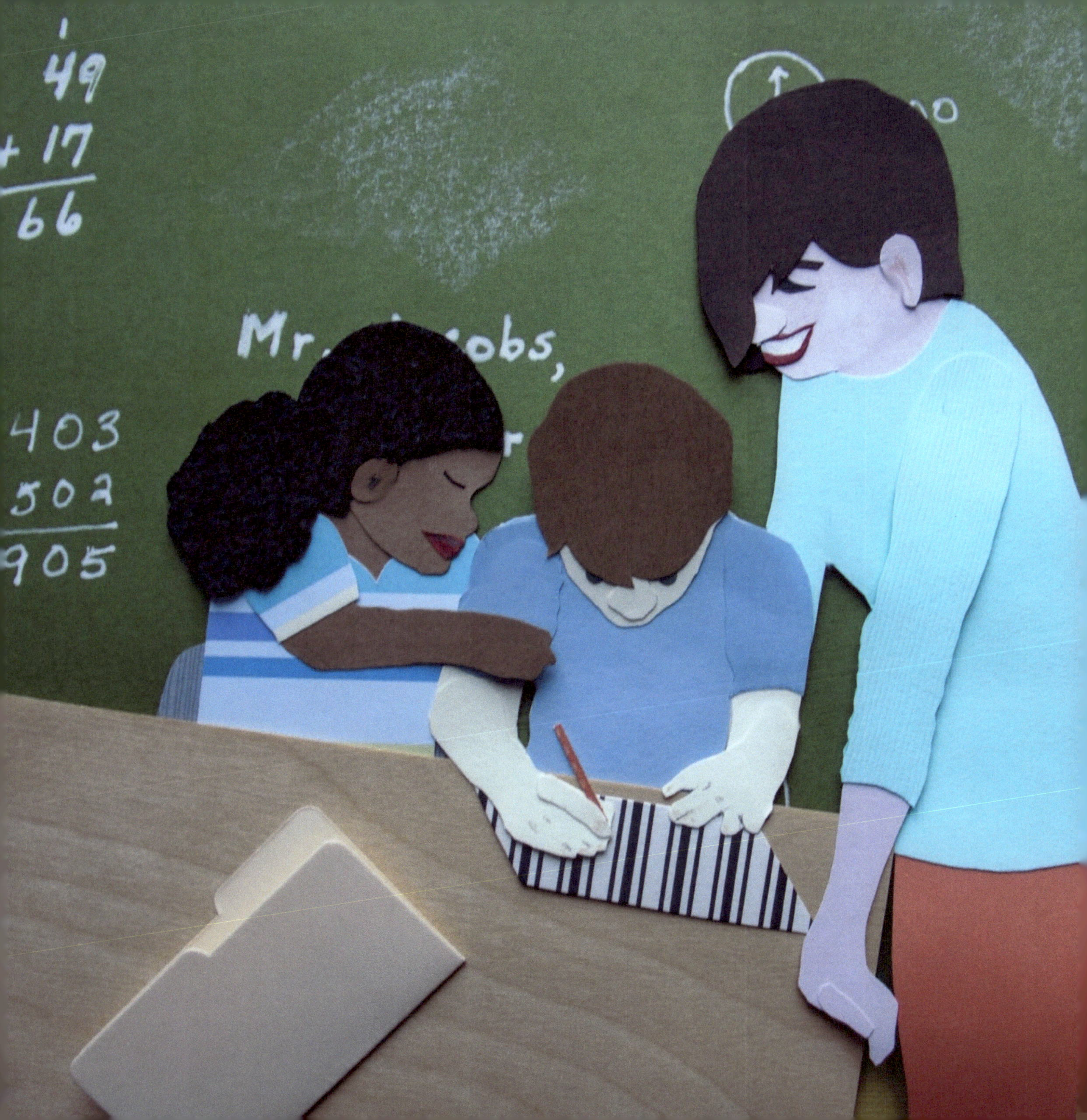
49
+ 17
66
Mr.
cobs,
403
502
905

Leah cannot walk.
She uses a wheelchair
and a special van to
get from here to there.

She likes to play, though,
and join in the fun.
She hates being left out,
feeling like the only one.

All of us feel different
so what should we do?
Ethan's Healthy Mind Express
has some advice for you.

There are friends aboard
to help all feel good
working together
as we all should.

The ride is full
of twists and turns
like the many choices
we face as we learn.

Jessa is a person
who is confident and poised.
She gets along well
with most girls and boys.

Hannah is scared
on the train ride.
Jessa points out
the beautiful countryside.

This made Hannah
smile again
because now she has
made a new friend.

Josh is funny and kind.
But Max can get mad with ease,
especially at someone
who likes to tease.

Josh shows Max
how to have a good time,
to ignore the bullies
so they aren't on his mind.

Some kids misbehave
when they want to be good.
They try to do well and
follow rules like they should.

Teachers are there
to meet face-to-face.
Teachers are one of many
that should provide a safe place.

There are parents, friends,
doctors, counselors, and nurses too,
policemen and leaders of faith,
whomever is comfortable for you.

Tell them your troubles.
Ask for advice.
Lean on them for support.
Their help should be nice.

When a friend may tell you
he's very sad,
it's always good
to tell your mom or dad.

Others can help
if you go to them and share.
This isn't tattling.
This shows that you care.

We have now come
to a bump in the track.
It's called the dark web,
but we cannot turn back.

Do not seek advice
even if they act like they care.
They still are strangers
so always beware.

CAUTION

SOME INTERNET
STORIES NOT
TRUE

Not everything you read
online is true.
Some people will tell you
wrong or unsafe things to do.

If you are confused,
ask someone you trust.
Confirming the truth
is always a must.

If Ethan's Healthy Mind Express
wants to stay on track each day,
it takes everyone on board
to listen, help, and do what they may.

We need to keep moving forward
without looking back.
It's not just the train;
it's really the track.

Ethan's Healthy Mind Express

A Children's First Mental Health Primer

ATTENTION!
RAILWAY SAFETY RULES

1 Nothing replaces human physical contact. Please take the time to always meet face-to-face. (F2F).

2 Respect starts with me. Nurture self-respect and respect for others. Strive to help others who find this a challenge. Think positive reinforcement versus rejection.

3 Avoid the Dark Web. Beware of areas that may be dangerous or lead to isolation.

4 Do not believe everything you see on social media.

5 We ALL need to Come Aboard! Family, clergy, friends, teachers, community members and those in the media. The goal is changing the tracks to meet everyone's needs. We Are All On This Ride Together.

About the Contributors:

Author Emily Lane Waszak is a writer in Michigan. She holds a B.A. in English from Michigan State University and an M.A. in Humanities from Central Michigan University. Emily's five children have inspired her passion to help the youth of today become the productive and healthy adults of tomorrow. She and Erik Bean have co-authored several academic books together.

Co-Author Erik Bean (Ethan's dad) holds a B.S. in Psychology from Grand Valley State University, an M.A. in Journalism from Michigan State University, and an Ed.D. from University of Phoenix and has co-authored academic books with Emily. He and wife Stacey, L.M.S.W. started the Ethan Bean Mental Wellness Foundation in 2019. Their daughter Blair is studying organizational leadership at Michigan State University class of 2020 and helps in all facets of the foundation.

Editor Sherry Wexler holds an M.S.W. from Wayne State University and is an advocate for atypicals. It is her hope that this book serves as a first step in changing our current culture to one that it is less competitive and that is more focused on acceptance and inclusion as this may decrease rates of anxiety and depression that many students both typical and atypical currently display.

Illustrator Gail Gorske, a full-time tutor, holds a B.A. in Education from Adrian College, with concentrations in math and art, and has taught second and third grade. Every day she strives to fit in creative endeavors – especially those involving paper arts. Gail and her husband love to travel with their two dogs. She credits her parents for giving her a love of art and healthy outlook on life.

Ethan Bean Mental Wellness Foundation

Mission
The Ethan Bean Mental Wellness Foundation is dedicated to examining the efficacy of ongoing mental health treatment, drug intervention, effects of social media, use of technology, and socialization in order to help remove societal stigma and improve acceptance/tolerance of those with mental health conditions as well as those that are uniquely lined. The goal is to learn better ways to support those who are different and accept them for their everyday obstacles. EthanBean.org, a Michigan 501(c)3 Non-Profit.

Web: EthanBean.org
Email: EthansMentalHealth@gmail.com
Phone: (248) 270-2974

www.ingramcontent.com/pod-product-compliance
Lightning Source LLC
Chambersburg PA
CBHW041540240626
47164CB00002B/76